前　　言

　　語言的學習，愈早愈好。孩子的模仿力強、吸收能力佳，小孩子的發音在還沒有形成地方口音之前，就讓他學習說英語，可避免晚一天學，多一天困難的煩惱！外國語言的學習與刺激，有助於智力的開發，及見聞的增長。前教育部次長阮大年說：「早學英語的好處很多。我小學四年級就開始學英語，以致到了台灣唸中學，我一直名列前茅。」

　　英語是「容易學習，很難學好」的語言。雖然容易學習，方法不得要領，也等於徒勞。「學習兒童美語讀本」設計活潑而有趣的學習方式，讓兒童快快樂樂地學會說英語。

◉ **對小朋友而言**：學習身邊的英語，能使兒童在開始學習英語時，有最直接而深刻的體驗。本套書以日常生活經常遇到的狀況為中心，提供一切能引起兒童興趣的學習題材。實用、生動而有創意的教材，讓孩子能自然親近趣味盎然的英語！

◉ **對教學者而言**：本套書編序完整、內容循序漸進，教學者易於整理。各頁教材之下，均有教學提示，可供老師參考，不必多花時間，就可獲得事半功倍的準備效果。本套書也針對兒童學習心理，每單元均有唱歌、遊戲，或美勞，使教學者能在輕鬆愉快的方式下，順利教學！

◉ **對父母親而言**：本套書的各單元均以日常生活為背景，也適合讓父母親來親自教導。在兒童心理學上，「親子教學法」對孩子學習能力的增強，有很大的幫助。本套書在每單元之後，均附有在家學習的方法，提供具體的方法和技巧，可以幫助家長與子女的共同學習！

　　透過這套書，兒童學習英語的過程，必然是輕鬆而愉快。而且，由於開始時所引發的興趣，未來的學習將會充滿興奮與期待！

本書的特色

- 學習語言的基本順序，是由Hearing（聽）、Speaking（說）、Reading（讀）、Writing（寫），本套教材即依此原則編輯。

- 內容背景本土化、國情化，使兒童在熟悉的環境中學習英語，以避免像其他的原文兒童英語書，與現實生活有出入的弊端。

- 題材趣味化、生活化，學了立即能在日常生活中使用。

- 將英語歌曲、遊戲，具有創意的美勞，與學習英語巧妙地組合在一起，以提高兒童的學習興趣，達到寓教於樂的目的。

- 每單元教材的形式一致，有效學習，方便教學。在書末並附有詳細的本書學習內容一覽表，查閱方便。

- 每單元的教材均有教學指導和提示，容易教學。而且每單元之末均列有目標說明，指導者易於掌握重點。

- 提供在家學習的方法，家長們可親自教導自己的子女學習英語，除加強親子關係外，也達到自然的學習成效。

- 每單元終了，附有考查學習成果的習作，有助於指導者了解學生的吸收力。

- 書末附有單元總複習，並收錄所有的生字圖，以加深學習印象。另外，在下一冊書的前面部分也有各種方式的複習，以達到溫故知新的目的。

- 本套書是以六歲兒童到國一學生為對象，內容自成一系統，可供不同程度的學習。

CONTENTS

Review 1

A. How many ?
(number and vocabulary review)

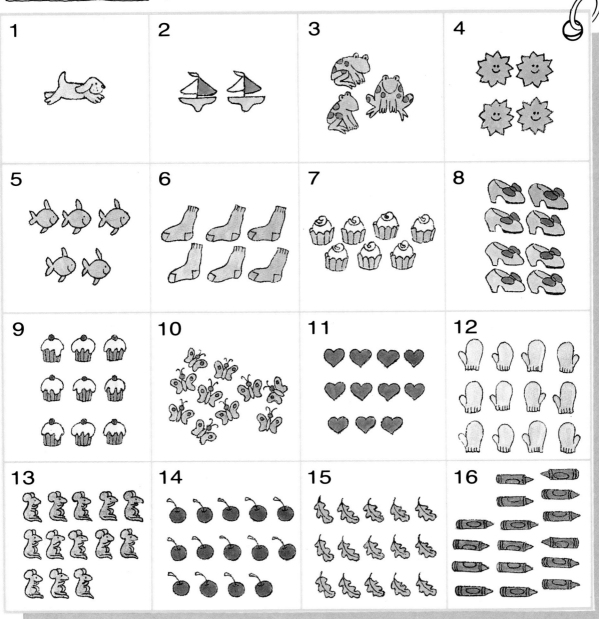

Note: Review the numbers one to one hundred. This may be done by using some simple and well known objects. Then teach the numbers with the words given on this page. A number of games are possible for reviewing numbers, clapping hands a number of times, guessing the number of beans in your hand, and oral arithmetic are useful ways for practicing numbers. These can also be played as team games.

Review 1   B. What time is it ?

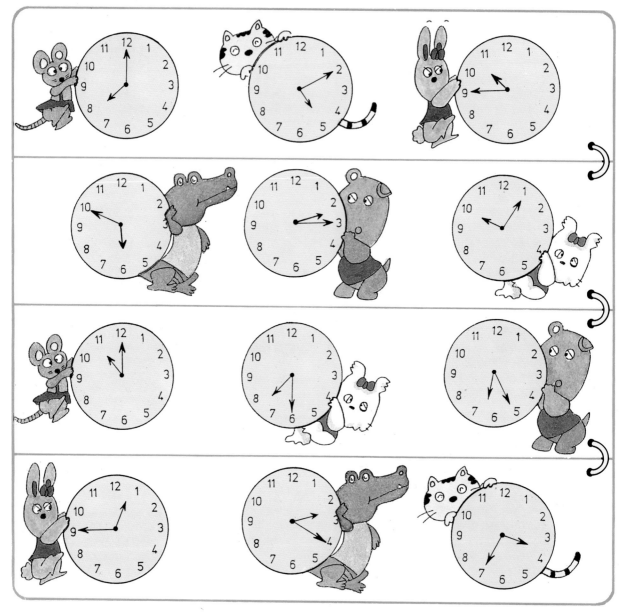

Note : Using either a clock-face with moveable hands, which can easily be
made, or drawings on the blackboard, review the following patterns:

1. It is ____ o'clock.
2. It is ____ -thirty.
3. It is _____（點）_____（分）.

Review 2

A. What is this?

1 A: Look at number one. What is this?
B: This is a flower.
A: Is this a flower ?
B: Yes. This is a flower.
2 A: Look at number two. What is this?
B: This is a car.
A: Is this a bicycle ?
B: No. This is a car.

Note: Practice using the first conversation with all of the pictures on this page. First, take the part of A and choose different students to take the part of B. Then have two students as A and B. After the first conversation, repeat this procedure using the second conversation model. If time permits, the same conversations may be used with other pictures or objects in the classroom.

Review 2 | B. What is that ?

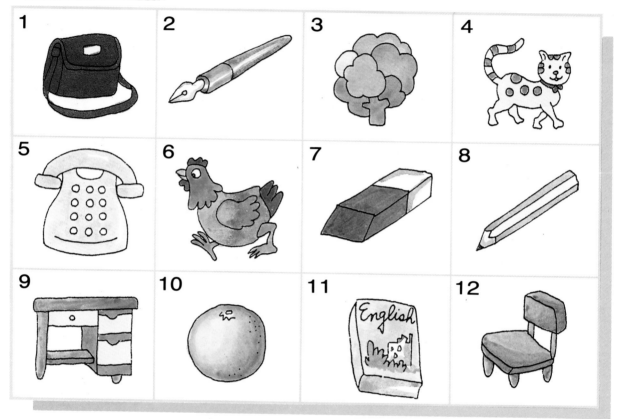

1. A: Look at number one. What is that ?
   B: That is a bag.
   A: Is that a bag ?
   B: Yes. That is a bag.
2. A: Look at number two. What is that ?
   B: That is a pen.
   A: Is that a pencil ?
   B: No. That is a pen.

Note: Follow the procedure outlined on the previous page. It is important that the two students are the same distance away from the object being pointed at. Remember to stress the distinction between "this" and "that", and have each student use the correct word for the situation.

Review 2

C. Touch and say:
This is my_____.

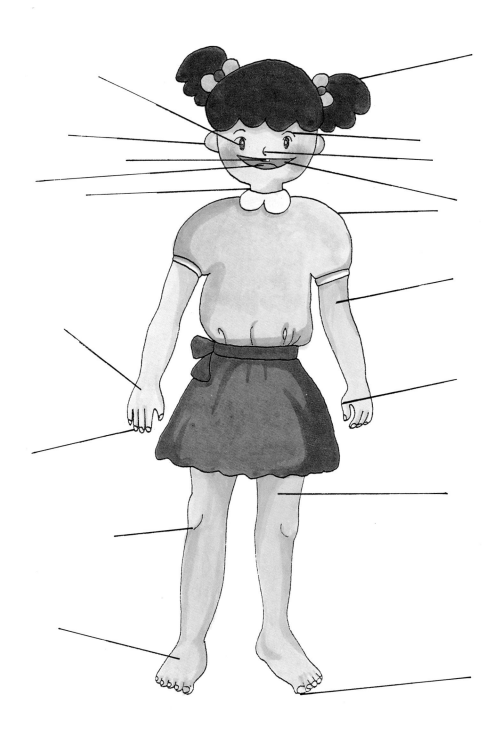

 **Review 3** A. I am/You are

I am John.
I am a boy.

I am Mary.
I am a girl.

You are Mary.
You are a girl.

You are John.
You are a boy.

I am Mr. Lee.
I am a man.

I am Miss Ling.
I am a woman.

You are Miss Ling.
You are a woman.

You are Mr. Lee.
You are a man.

Note: Bring some children to the front of the class. Point to yourself and say "I am Mr./Mrs./Miss_____. I am a man/woman." Then point to a child and say "You are_____. You are a boy/girl." Go around the class and say the sentences to each child. Have them reply with "I am_____. I am a boy/girl. You are Mr./Mrs./Miss _____. You are a man/woman." Finally, form a conversation chain to practice these patterns.

Review 3   B. He is/She is a

Note: Bring some students to the front of the classroom and review "He is a boy." and "She is a girl." Remember to point to the student as you review the sentences. Then, have the students practice with each other. Finally, use the pictures on this page to practice the sentences.

1. HELLO, HOW ARE YOU ?

Note : For these pages, have the children listen and repeat all together.
Then have volunteers role-play the dialogue for each page. Finally,
have the students role-play the two pages together.

LET'S PRACTICE
Look and say.

Note : These interesting pictures will help the children learn greetings.
Give them a simple explanation about each picture.

SING A SONG
Hello, How Are You?

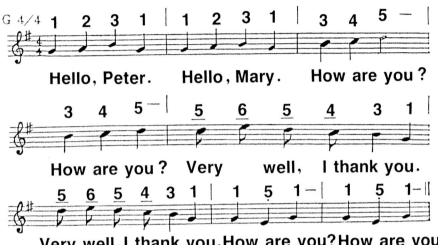

Note: The melody of this song is that of "Two Tigers". Remind your students of the melody by singing it to them first. Then, exchange the names of your students with those in the song. Finally, bring your students up to the front of the classroom, two at a time, and have them sing the song to each other and exchange greetings.

■ **本單元目標**：學習「你好嗎？」「很好，謝謝你。」等問候的方法。
　1. Hello. 隨時隨地都可說的一種問候用語。
　2. How are you？→ I am fine. Thank you.
■ **在家學習的方法**：首先，由媽媽先說 How are you, —（名字）？再由孩子回答 Fine, thank you, 反覆練習到流利之後，再依下列順序練習：
●子：How are you, Mummy？
●媽：I am fine, thank you. How are you, ～？
●子：I am fine, thank you.
順序可對調，練習至會話流利為止。

2. WHAT TIME IS IT ? (II)

a half

a quarter

It is **half** past six.

It is a **quarter** to ten.

LET'S PRACTICE
Look and say.

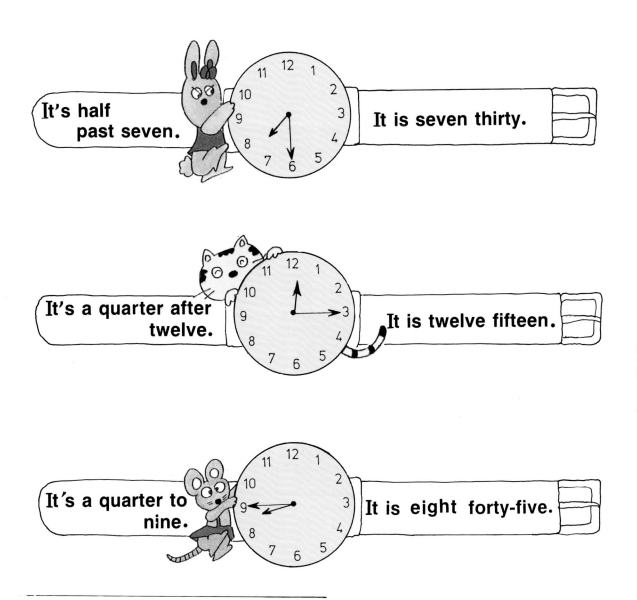

It's half past seven.

It is seven thirty.

It's a quarter after twelve.

It is twelve fifteen.

It's a quarter to nine.

It is eight forty-five.

Note : First, the teacher has to tell the students about the meanings of the two words (a half = thirty ; a quarter = fifteen). Make sure they really understand these two words. Then teach them how to use " after; to " correctly. You can do more practice in class. Write down some specific times on the blackboard and ask them to write down two answers.

PLAY A GAME
What time is it ?

Note : The teacher can bring a clock to the class. Let one student turn the
hands of the clock and ask, "What time is it ?". The student who
raises his hand first gets the chance to answer.

EXERCISE

A. Write and draw .

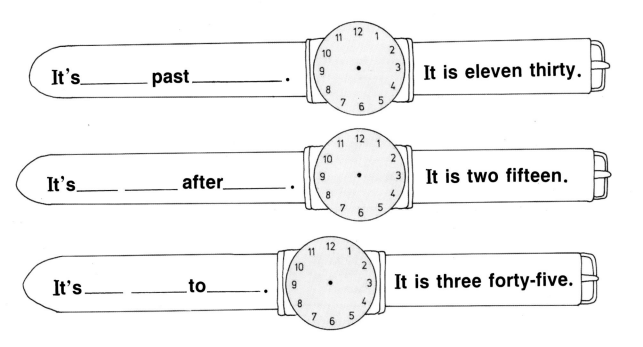

It's_____ past_____ .   It is eleven thirty.

It's____ _____ after_____ .   It is two fifteen.

It's____ _____to_____ .   It is three forty-five.

B. Fill in the blanks .

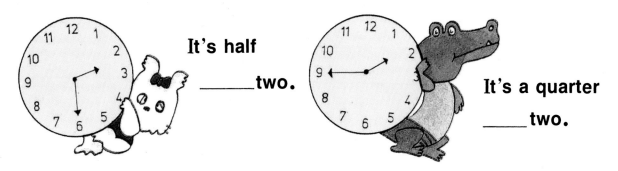

It's half _____two.

It's a quarter ____two.

■ 本單元目標：複習已教過的一些數字說法，和練習其他方式的時間表示法。
　　　　1. half 和 a quarter 的使用。
　　　　2. past, after 和 to 的使用。

■ 在家學習的方法：先教小朋友認識 half 和 quarter 這兩個字，然後利用家中的時鐘，教導他正確地使用 past, after 和 to。請隨時間小朋友 " What time is it?" 多次地反覆練習，能加深小朋友的印象。

3. HOW OLD ARE YOU ?
HOW TALL ARE YOU ?

John: How old are you, Mary ?
Mary: I'm 9 years old.
John: How tall are you?
Mary: I'm 120 centimeters tall.
John: How old is your sister ?
Mary: She's 12 years old.
John: How tall is she ?
Mary: She's 150 centimeters tall.

Note: 1. centimeter = c.m.

2. Teacher (to boy student): How old are you?
   Student: I am nine years old.
   Teacher (to class): He is nine years old.

3. Teacher (to girl student): How old are you?
   Student 1: I am ten years old.
   Teacher (to another student): How old is she?
   Student 2: She's ten years old.

Practice the model above with several more students. Then, use the model with "How tall are you?".

3-1 LET'S PRACTICE
Questions and answers.

Q: How old is your father ?

A: He's 40 years old.

Q: How tall is he ?

A: He's 170 centimeters tall.

3-2 SING A SONG
How old are you ?

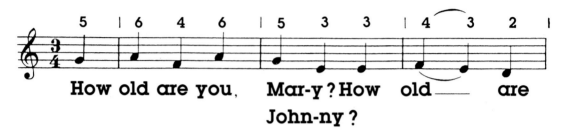

How old are you,　Mar-y ? How　old———　are
John-ny ?

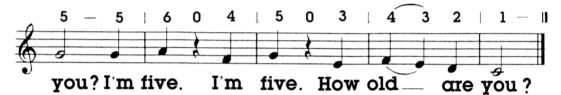

you ? I'm five.　I'm　five. How old———　are you ?
　　　six.　　　　six.

■ **本單元目標**：練習年齡及身高的問法與答法。
1. How old are you?　　I am ～ years old.
2. How tall are you?　　I am ～ centimeters tall.

■ **在家學習的方法**：反覆練習至孩子能流利地說出：I am ～ years old.；I am ～ centimeters tall. 之後，可以和爸、媽假設一個會話狀況共同作練習：

媽：How old are you, John?
子：I am ten years old.
父：How tall are you?
子：I am 120 centimeters tall. How old is Mother?
父：She is 35 years old.
子：How old is Father?
媽：He is 40 years old.

4. THERE IS A BLACKBOARD.

There is a blackboard.

There is a map.

There is a piano.

There is a clock.

There is a jar.

There is a door.

There is a teacher.

Note : Teach the pattern on this page using the method mentioned previously
and using familiar objects already taught. Please introduce the new
words: map and door.

4. THERE ARE FOUR BOOKS.

There are four books.

There are four desks.

There are four chairs.

There are two pictures.

There are two butterflies.

There are three students.

There are three pencilboxes.

There are four erasers.

There are four rulers.

There are nine pencils.

Note：Using just a few familiar objects, teach the pattern "There are _____." Pay particular attention to pronunciation here. Most plurals end in "s", but three pronunciations are possible.("s","z", and "ɪz").

LET'S PRACTICE
Point and say.

Note: Use this picture to practice
the patterns:
"There is a _____.", and
"There are _____.".

4-2 PLAY A GAME

Note: First, the teacher instructs the students to close their eyes or to turn around so that they can't see the teacher's desk. Next, place a number of articles on the teacher's desk and allow the students to see them briefly. Then cover them up or put them away. Finally, have the students recall what was on the desk using these patterns: "There is a＿＿＿.", and "There are number noun." Score points for each correct answer. This can be played on an individual or team basis.

EXERCISE
Look and write.

1 　How many boys are there?

　How many girls are there?

2 　How many lions are there?

3 　How many tigers are there?

4 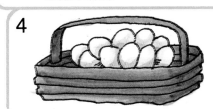　How many eggs are there?

5 　How many apples are there?

■**本單元目標**：學習「有多少～？」的說法。

How many ～ are there? $\begin{cases} \text{There is ～.} \\ \text{There are ～.} \end{cases}$

■**在家學習的方法**：先複習已教過的數字 1～100 之後，將英語名稱已知的東西，準備數種（數目最好不要相同），分類排列。準備好以後，可開始練習：

母：How many ～ are there?

子：There is(are) ～.

5. IS THERE A HOUSE?

Is there a house ?

　　Yes, there is.

Is there a farmer ?

　　No, there is not.

Is there a kite ?

Is there a car ?

Is there a river ?

Is there an airplane ?

Is there a bicycle ?

Is there a boat ?

Is there a cloud ?

Is there anything else ?

Note : First, provide a model by asking and answering several questions us-
ing familiar objects with the pattern "Is there _____ ?"
For example: Is there a blackboard? Yes, there is.
　　　　　　 Is there an elephant? No, there isn't.

5. ARE THERE TWO DOGS?

Are there two ducks?
  Yes, there are.
Are there four hens?
  No, there are not.
Are there three dogs?
Are there four boys?
Are there seven birds?
Are there six trees?
Are there two buses?
Are there three roads?
Are there four men?
Are there five girls?

Note: First, practice the pattern with objects in the classroom, then
have the students use the picture to ask and answer questions. Note
that it is best to teach the full form "No, there is/are not."
first and then "No, there isn't/aren't.".

LET'S PRACTICE
Questions and answers.

5-1

1.
duck
boy
hen
lion
fish

2.
bird
kite
girl
flower
rabbit

3.
umbrella
table
cat
zebra
violin

4.
ship
airplane
sun
car
bird

5.
chair
door
picture
bus
desk

Note : First, have the children circle the words that they can find in the picture. Then practice questions and answers using "Is there a _____ ?" with each student.

PLAY A GAME
Do and say.

Note: Put some things in a big bag, and select a student to play Santa Claus. The Santa should remember what is in the bag. Next, tell the rest of the children to think about something that they want, and have them ask Santa Claus. Use the pattern: "Is there a____?" The Santa should answer with either "yes" or "no". If someone guesses right, the child will be given that object.

5-3 EXERCISE

A. Look and answer.

1. Is there a bag? _____.

2. Is there a rabbit? _____.

3. Are there three cats? _____.

4. Are there four balls? _____.

B. Look and draw.

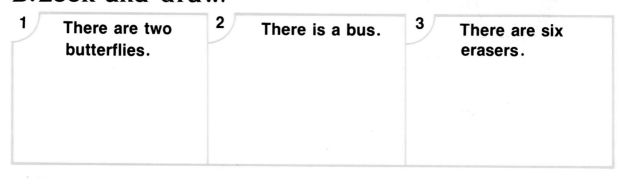

1　There are two butterflies.

2　There is a bus.

3　There are six erasers.

■ **本單元目標**：學習「有沒有」的問法與答法。
  1. Is there a ~ ?　Yes, there is.　No, there is not.
  2. Are there ~ ?　Yes, there are.　No, there are not.

■ **在家學習的方法**：以書上的那幅圖來練習 Is there ~ ?；Are there ~ ?的問法與答法。肯定與否定要兼顧練習。然後，媽媽將許多東西放進一個袋子裏，讓小孩以 "Is there a ~ ?" 的問法來猜猜看有那些東西。反之，讓媽媽來猜亦可，以增加親子學習樂趣。

6. DAYS AND MONTHS

Sunday

Monday

Tuesday

Wednesday

Thursday

Friday

Saturday

What day is today?

It is Monday.

Note : Use a calendar or pictures to present and practice the days of the
week and the months of the year. Point to the days and the months
and have the class recite these in chorus.

LET'S PRACTICE
Learn these rhymes.

Solomon Grundy
Solomon Grundy,
Born on Monday,
Christened on Tuesday,
Married on Wednesday,
Taken ill on Thursday,
Worse on Friday,
Died on Saturday,
Buried on Sunday,
this is the end
Of Solomon Grundy.

Thirty Days Hath September
Thirty days hath September,
April, June, and November;
All the rest have thirty-one,
Save February,
    which has twenty-eight in fine,
And leap year brings it twenty-nine.

SING A SONG
Days of a week.

Sun- day la- la- la, Mon-day la- la- la,

Tues-day la- la- la, Wednes-day,

Thurs-day la- la- la, Fri- day la- la- la,

Sat-ur-day. That makes a week.

EXERCISE
Fill in the blanks.

(A) A week.

(B) A year.

February

■**本單元目標**：學習星期及月份的名稱。

■**在家學習的方法**：利用書上的插圖反複練習各種星期和月份的說法。然後再以日曆和月曆來做實際練習。

7. WHAT IS IT ?

1. What is it ?

It is a candy.

2. What is it ?

It is a banana.

3. What is it ?

It is a picture.

4. What is it ?

It is a doll.

5. What is it ?

It is a radio.

6. What is it ?

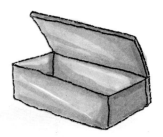

It is a box.

Note: Teach these new words in this way: First, have the students repeat after the teacher. Then ask the students what each one is. Teach the students to ask "What is it?" Finally, have the students take turns asking each other questions. Each student should point to a picture when asking the question. This can be made into a team game.

1. Is this a bicycle ?

Yes, it is.

It is a bicycle.

2. Is this a telephone ?

No, it is not.

It is not a telephone.

It is a television.

3. Is that an airplane ?

Yes, it is.

It is an airplane.

4. Is that a door ?

No, it is not.

It is not a door.

It is a window.

5. Is it a cup ?

No, it is not.

It is not a cup.

It is a glass.

6. Is it a cap ?

Yes, it is.

It is a cap.

Note: Use objects, pictures, or board drawings for asking and answering questions. Teach the students to ask questions by repeating after you. Special care should be taken in distinguishing between near and far objects. Games are very useful for language practice. Use the game listed in the previous lesson as a model, but make sure that the students have sufficient practice in asking and answering questions.

LET'S PRACTICE
Look and say.

1.

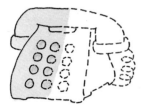

Is this a telephone ?

Yes, it is.

It is a  .

2.

Is this a fish?

No, it is not.

It is not a

It is an 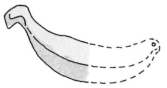 .

3.

Is this a ruler ?

No, it is not.

It is not a 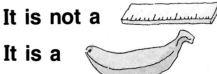 .

It is a 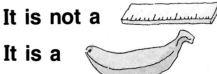 .

4.

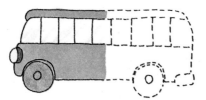

Is this a bus ?

Yes, it is.

It is a  .

5.

Is this an egg ?

No, it is not.

It is not an

It is a  .

SING A SONG

Is this a book ?

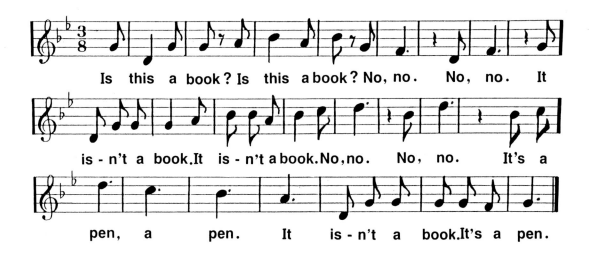

Note : Use a pen as a prop when teaching this song. Remember that any familiar nouns can be substituted for book and pen. Next, display a group of familiar picture cards on the table. Let the students go up to the table individually or in pairs, pick up the pictures, and sing the question. Remind the students to name the picture incorrectly, and that the answer must always be: "No, no." Sing this song throughout the year to reinforce old and new vocabulary.

 **7-3** **EXERCISE**

A. Join, write and say.

1

It is a _____ .

2

_____ .

3

_____ .

B. Draw and write.

1 **Draw a box.**

It is a _____ .

2 **Draw a butterfly.**

_____ .

3 **Draw a window.**

_____ .

■**本單元目標**：學習 it 的用法。
　　What is it（this, that）？　It is a～.
　　Is it（this, that）a～？　Yes,～.　No,～.
■**在家學習的方法**：利用已熟悉的事物、或書上的圖來作問與答的反覆練習。並以各種距離的問法來使其熟練 it 的用法。

8. THESE ARE PEARS.
THOSE ARE PEARS.

Note : First review " This is a_____. " and " That is a_____. " using familiar classroom objects. For " This is a_____. " use an object that the students already have on their desks and can touch while they are speaking. For " That is a_____. " use any object that they know that is placed some distance from them.

Note: Teach "These are _____." and "Those are _____." using the same method with more than one object. Lastly, read the pictures and teach the new words on these two pages.

LET'S PRACTICE
Look and say.

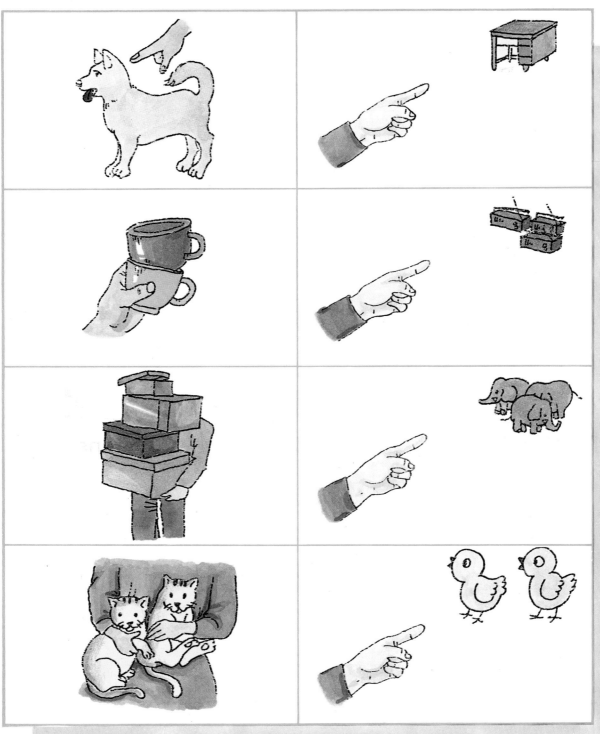

8-2 PLAY A GAME
Hangman

Note: First, divide the whole class into two groups and have each team pick a word. Have each team tell you the word in private and put the appropriate number of blanks on the board. (One for each letter of the word). Each team then takes turns guessing letters. If they are right, then fill in the appropriate blank with the letter. If they are wrong, write the wrong letter under the row of blanks and draw one part of the hang-man (a simple stick figure drawing). Continue until either a whole figure is completed or the word is guessed. To score points, one team must guess the other team's word, regardless of who has the completed hang-man.

EXERCISE
Look at the pictures and make sentences.

■ **本單元目標**：學習「這些是～。」「那些是～。」等複數的說法。
1. This is a ～. → These are ～.
2. That is a ～. → Those are ～.

■ **在家學習的方法**：首先，請準備幾樣不同的物品，每種至少兩個以上。先拿出一個物品，練習 This is a ～. 再拿出另外幾個同樣的物品來反覆練習 These are ～. That 和 Those 的練習方式也是一樣，但要注意將東西放遠一些。

9.  WHAT ARE THESE (THOSE)?

What are these ?

Are these ducks ?	No, they are not.
Are these hens ?	No, they are not.
Are these chickens?	Yes, they are.
	They are chickens.

What are these ?

Are these lions ?	No, they are not.
Are these zebras ?	No, they are not.
Are these pigs ?	Yes, they are.
	They are pigs.

What are these ?

Are these sticks ?	No, they are not.
Are these rulers ?	No, they are not.
Are these keys ?	Yes, they are.
	They are keys.

What are these ?

Are these pens ?	No, they are not.
Are these keys ?	No, they are not.
Are these knives ?	Yes, they are.
	They are knives.

Note : First use familiar objects to teach students to ask questions as well as answer them. Then use the pictures on this page, or any other pictures available, to introduce and practice new words.

What are those ?

Are those airplanes? No, they are not.

Are those birds? No, they are not.

Are those clouds? Yes, they are.

They are clouds.

What are those ?

Are those pigs? No, they are not.

Are those babies? No, they are not.

Are those monkeys? Yes, they are.

They are monkeys.

What are those ?

Are those bags? No, they are not.

Are those boxes? No, they are not.

Are those baskets? Yes, they are.

They are baskets.

What are those ?

Are those clocks? No, they are not.

Are those violins? No, they are not.

Are those watches? Yes, they are.

They are watches.

Note: Many games are available for practicing these patterns. One game, which children love, is for the teacher to turn her back to the whole class and have one student choose an object or a picture and show it to the rest of the class. The teacher then tries to guess what it is by asking the class "yes" or "no" questions.

9-1 LET'S PRACTICE

Questions and answers.

Q: What are these ?
A: They're apples.
Q: What are those ?
A: They're oranges.

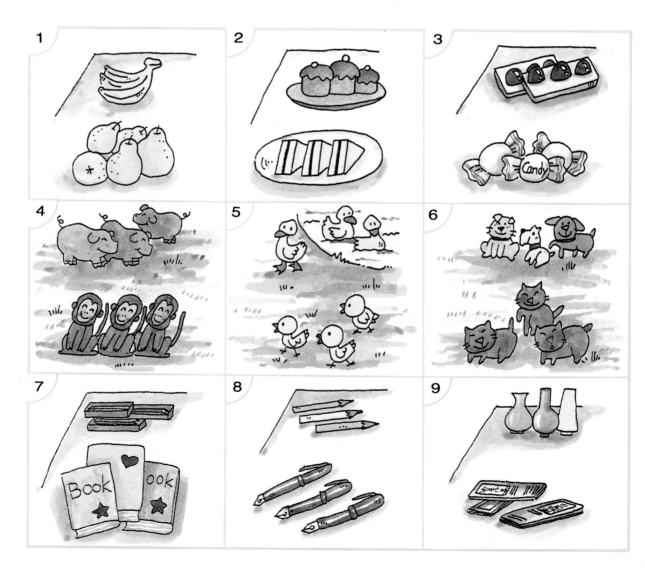

PLAY A GAME

Hit the bat.

Note : First, put some things in a box so that there are at least two of
each thing. Then draw a square on the board such as the one above
and divide the whole class into two teams. Have each team pick a
number from 1 to 9 as their "danger" numbers. A representative
from each team should inform you in secret of the number. Next,
bring one child from each of the teams to the front of the class.
Then take something out of the box and ask what it is. The child
who raises his or her hand first gets to answer. They should say:
"They are＿＿＿." If he/she is right then they get to pick a number; if the answer is wrong then the question is deferred to the
other team. Continue until one of them hits the danger number.

EXERCISE

Write and read: What are these ?

They are _____ .

_____ .

_____ .

_____ .

■ **本單元目標**：學習「這些是～嗎？」「那些是～嗎？」的問法與答法。

　1. Are these ～ ?　　Yes, they are.　　No, they are not.

　2. Are those ～ ?　　Yes, they are.　　No, they are not.

■ **在家學習的方法**：以書上的插圖或家中的東西來練習這些句型。要注意所問的事物之遠近，而有 these 和 those 的區別。

10. WHAT IS YOUR FATHER?

John: What is your father ?
Mary: He is a doctor.
John: Is your mother a teacher ?
Mary: No, she isn't. She isn't a teacher.
John: What is she ?
Mary: She is a typist.

Note: First, ask the students: "What is your father/mother?" to let them practice the answers about their occupations. After each one can speak fluently, let them do a role-play as in the dialogue.

1 He is a pilot.

2 She is a stewardess.

3 He is a sailor.

4 She is a housewife.

5 He is a fireman.

6 He is a driver.

7 He is a baker.

8 She is a waitress.

Note: Read the occupations listed on this page while the students look at the pictures. Give more practice by using simple drawings on the board. Pick some representative items from some occupation and repeat the occupation as you draw the objects on the board. Then, point to the symbols of the occupations and have the students say: "He is a doctor/teacher/farmer/etc." Extend this out by having a boy, and a girl come up and do a role-play. Ask the class: "What is she/he?" and have them respond with "He/She is a_____."

LET'S PRACTICE

Questions and answers.

Q: Who am I ?

A: You are a mailman.

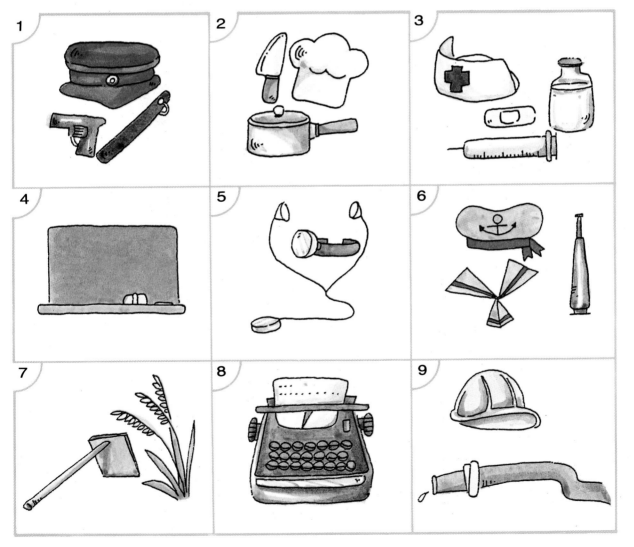

1

2

3

4

5

6

7

8

9

PLAY A GAME
A crossword puzzle.

10-3 EXERCISE
Look and say.

■ **本單元目標**：學習各種職業的說法、及詢問的方法。

What is your ～?

■ **在家學習的方法**：首先，媽媽先問孩子What is your father? What is your mother? 讓他能熟悉地回答He is a～. She is a～. 為止。然後利用課本上的插圖來反覆練習各行各業的說法。

11. COLORS (1)

This is a train. It is blue.

**This is a rabbit.
It is white.**

**This is a balloon.
It is purple.**

**This is an apple.
It is red.**

**This is a banana.
It is yellow.**

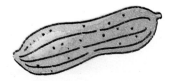

**This is a cucumber.
It is green.**

**This is a hat.
It is black.**

Note: Teach the seven colors with the above sentence pattern and using classroom objects. Do both teacher-student and student-student dialogues. Touch or point to an object and say: "This is a_____." and have the other one say "It is_____".

1 What color is this car ?    It is red.

2 What color is this book ?    It is green.

3 What color is this desk ? 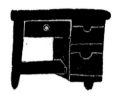   It is black.

4 What color is this dog ?    It is white.

5 What color is this ball ?   It is blue.

6 What color is this duck ?    It is yellow.

7 What color is this umbrella ?    It is purple.

Note: Either have the teacher ask the questions and have the class re-
     spond, or have the students ask each other.

LET'S PRACTICE
Circle and say.

1. This car is
green
red   and
black

that car is
yellow.
blue.
white.

2. This ball is
yellow
blue   and
green

that ball is
purple.
red.
white.

3. This train is
black
purple   and
white

that train is
green.
blue.
red.

4. This cat is
black
yellow   and
white

that cat is
purple.
blue.
black.

Note: For props you should have identical objects of different colors.
Demonstrate with: "This pen is _____ and that pen is _____." Be
sure to distinguish between near and far objects with "this" and
"that". Continue this pattern with other objects.

SING A SONG
What color is for you?

Red, pur - ple, green and blue, green and blue, green and blue

Brown, black and yel - low, too. What col - or is for you?

Note: Use this song as a color review game. First, make small cards
or slips of paper; one set with colors and the other with the
names of the colors. Place the word cards in a box and the color
ones on the chalk tray. Then, have the students form a circle
and skip around the box as they sing. Let a volunteer pick a card
from the box and sing the question: "What color is for you?" The
student must read the card and pick out the correct color card
from the chalk tray, and then name at least one object in the
room that is also that color. Finally, have the student put the
card back in the box, and ask for another volunteer. Continue with
the game until everyone has had a turn.

EXERCISE
11-3
Color and write.

Color this ball purple.
Color that ball green.

This ball is_____.   **This ball is_____.**

Color this train blue
and color that train purple.

_____.   _____.

Color this cat black
and color that cat brown.

_____.   _____.

Color this book red
and color that book yellow.

_____.   _____.

■**本單元目標**：學習顏色的說法。What color is this～？→ It is～.

■**在家學習的方法**：一面看著書上的圖畫，一面逐一發問What color is this～？並且回答 It is～.等。能夠發問與回答以後，就讓子女把彩色筆拿出來，逐一說 This is～. 在平時，更要隨時隨地給予練習機會，以熟悉各事物顏色的說法。

12. COLORS (2)

1.

What color is milk ?
Milk is white.

2.

What color is tea ?
Tea is black.

3.

What color is bread ?
Bread is white.

4.

What color is grass ?
Grass is green.

5.

What color is rice ?
Rice is white.

6.

What color is coffee ?
Coffee is brown.

Note: Try to have some samples of the objects above. The teacher should
  ask the questions and the students should repeat the answers after
  the teacher. Note that we don't say "a milk," as it is an uncountable
  noun. Either the teacher can ask the questions and have the students answer, or the students can ask each other questions.

1.

**Is this a blue book
or a purple book ?**

It is a blue book.

2.

**Is this a white elephant
or a gray elephant ?**

It is a gray elephant.

3.

**Is this a red ball
or an orange ball ?**

It is an orange ball.

4.

**Is this an orange car
or a yellow car ?**

It is a yellow car.

5.

**Is this a brown desk
or a green desk ?**

It is a brown desk.

6.

**Is this a red telephone
or a pink telephone ?**

It is a pink telephone.

Note: First, teach the three colors — gray, orange, and pink using familiar objects. Then, teach questions with "or" as in the above patterns. Give more practice by using classroom objects. The students
should practice the questions as well as the answers.

12-1 LET'S PRACTICE
Ask and answer.

What color is it ?

It is green.

Is it a tree ?

No.

Is it grass ?

Yes.

Note: First, practice with chorus work. Then have each student ask other
students for his/her chosen object. Finally, divide the whole class
into two groups for a team game.

SING A SONG
Colors

12-2

1 Red,   yel- low, blue, and green
2 Pink,   pur- ple, brown, and tan stand   up.
3 Gold   sil-ver, black, and white

Red,   yel-low, blue, and green
Pink,   pur-ple, brown, and tan turn a- round and
Gold,   sil-ver, black, and white

stretch up   high   a- bove your heads.   Oh,

Red,   yel-low, blue, and green
Pink,   pur-ple, brown, and tan sit   down.
Gold,   sil-ver, black, and white

Note : Give each child the name of a different color. Then, explain to
them what the actions "stand up", "turn around and stretch up high
above your head", and "sit down" mean. When the whole class can
sing the song and name the colors, then the children who have those
colors should do the appropriate actions as they sing. If someone
does it wrong, then he/she is out.

EXERCISE
Read the sentences and color the picture.

1. This airplane is gray.

2. This kite is green.

3. This river is blue.

4. This duck is yellow.

5. This fish is orange.

6. This umbrella is purple.

7. This pig is pink.

8. This dog is brown.

9. This zebra is black and white.

10. This bicycle is red.

■ **本單元目標**：學習顏色以及一些不可數的物質名詞的說法。

■ **在家學習的方法**：按照前單元的方式反覆練習各種東西顏色的說法。尤其要注意，不可數的物質前面不可加 a 或 an。

13. SIZES

1.

This mouse is **little**.
This elephant is **big**.

2.

This fox is **thin**.
This bear is **fat**.

3.

This girl is **short**.
This boy is **tall**.

Note: Teach little/big first, using objects or drawings on the board.
(For example: "The bag is little". "The hat is big.") When the
students have become accustomed to using this sentence pattern,
teach the next two pairs of sizes using the pictures in this book.

4.

This banana is **short**. This banana is **long**.

5.

This door is **narrow**. This door is **wide**.

6.

This book is **thin**. This book is **thick**.

Note: Now teach the new sizes on this page by using familiar objects like books, rulers, pencils, windows, etc. Notice that it is often necessary to teach sizes in contrasting pairs in order to bring out the meaning.

LET'S PRACTICE
Three rhymes.

(1) Little Tommy Tucker

Little Tommy Tucker
Sings for his supper.
What shall he eat?
White bread and butter.
How will he cut it
Without any knife?
How will he be married
Without any wife?

(2) The Little Girl with the Curl

There was a little girl.
Who had a little curl
Right in the middle of her forehead.
When she was good.
She was very, very good,
But when she was bad
She was horrid.

(3) Little Nanny Etticoat (A Riddle)

Little Nanny Etticoat

In a white petticoat

And a red nose;

The longer she stands

The shorter she grows. (A Candle)

SING A SONG
THIS LITTLE PIG WENT TO MARKET.

13-2

C
This lit-tle pig went to mar-ket.

G (wiggle child's big toe)
This lit-tle pig stayed at home.

C (wiggle second toe)
This lit-tle pig had —— roast beef.

F (wiggle third toe)
This lit-tle pig had —— none. And

C (wiggle fourth toe)   F
this lit-tle pig cried, "Wee—wee—wee—wee—wee,"

C   G   C (wiggle little toe)
All the way home.

13-3 EXERCISE

A. Circle the correct picture.

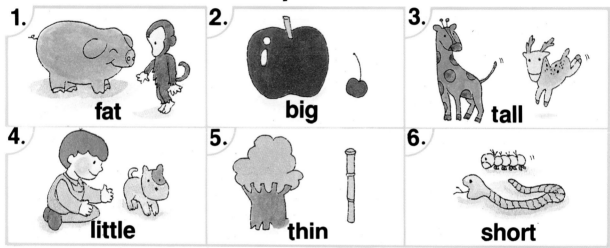

1. fat
2. big
3. tall
4. little
5. thin
6. short

B. Circle and read.

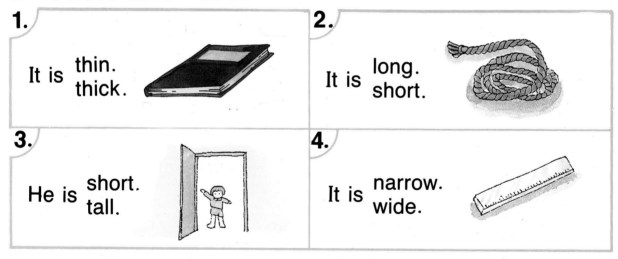

1. It is thin. / thick.
2. It is long. / short.
3. He is short. / tall.
4. It is narrow. / wide.

■ **本單元目標**：學習「大的」、「小的」、「長的」、「短的」、「寬的」、「窄的」、「厚的」、「薄的」等表示東西的形狀的字，以及「高的」、「矮的」、「胖的」、「瘦的」等形容人的外觀的字。

■ **在家學習的方法**：首先，請準備幾樣大小、長短、寬窄、厚薄不同的同樣物品。例如：長鉛筆和短鉛筆，反覆練習This pencil is long（short）．以及其他形狀的物品。並以形狀相反的問句來使其熟練各種形狀的說法。另外，以書中的人物，或家人來作高矮胖瘦等相同的練習。

14. ADJECTIVES

1.

This is a **young** man.

2.

This is not a **young** man. He is **old**.

3.

This is a **new** car.

4.

This is not a **new** car. It is **old**.

5.

This is a **clean** shirt.

6.

This is not a **clean** shirt. It is **dirty**.

Note: Teach the sentences using the illustrations in the book. Let them be familiar with the positive and negative forms.

7.

This is a **pretty** girl.

8.

This is not a **pretty** girl.
She is **ugly**.

9.

This is a **happy** girl.

10.

This is not a **happy** boy.
He is **sad**.

11.

This is a **hungry** woman.

12.

This is not a **hungry** man.
He is **thirsty**.

LET'S PRACTICE
Questions and answers.

PLAY A GAME
Bring me a new eraser.

Note: Divide the class into three groups. Have the groups stand an equal distance from you and draw a line on the floor to prevent them from coming nearer. Then appoint a runner in each team to bring the objects you ask for, e.g. "Bring me a new eraser.". The first runner to bring you the eraser gets a point. Then, ask for other objects. The first group to get five points wins. If you wish to make it more difficult for the class, ask for a number of objects.

14-3 EXERCISE

A. Look and draw.

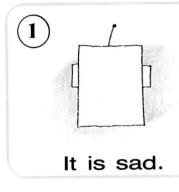

① It is sad.

② She is happy.

③ He is ugly.

B. Make sentences.

① _____.

② _____.

③ _____.

④ _____.

■**本單元目標**：學習表示東西的性質──「新的」、「舊的」；人的外觀──「年輕的」、「年老的」、「美的」、「醜的」、「乾淨的」、「髒的」；以及人的感覺──「餓的」、「渴的」、「快樂的」、「傷心的」等各種形容詞。

■**在家學習的方法**：以書上的各個圖畫來作練習，並不斷以肯定、否定的問題來確使其熟練。更重要的是，平常即能隨時隨地來問 Are you hungry（thirsty,...）?

Review | Point and say.
At the zoo.

 **Review** # Look and write. # (Free composition.)

_____

_____

_____

_____

_____

_____

Review Look, draw and color.

Draw a big apple.

Draw a thin farmer.

Draw a little cat.

Draw a beautiful butterfly.

Draw a dirty pig.

Draw a happy driver.

Color the sun orange.
Color the clouds white and blue.
Color the birds yellow and purple.
Color the tree green.
Color the windows brown and yellow.
Color the house white.
Color the car red and black.
Color the hens orange.
Color the chickens yellow.

Color the grass green.
Color the flowers pink.
Color the fish orange.
Color the river blue.
Color the mouse gray.
Color the apple red.
Color the cat black.
Color the pig pink.
Color the butterfly yellow.

Picture dictionary

1. an airplane	2. a baker	3. a balloon	4. a banana
5. a basket	6. a boat	7. a box	8. bread
9. a bus	10. a butterfly	11. a candy	12. a cap
13. chalk	14. a chicken	15. a cloud	16. coffee
17. a cookie	18. a cucumber	19. a doll	20. a door

21. a driver	**22.** a fireman	**23.** a fly	**24.** a glass
25. grass	**26.** a housewife	**27.** a key	**28.** a knife
29. a map	**30.** milk	**31.** a monkey	**32.** a mouse
33. a pear	**34.** a pencil box	**35.** a picture	**36.** a pig
37. a pilot	**38.** a radio	**39.** rice	**40.** a river

41. a road

42. a sailor

43. a stewardess

44. tea

45. a television

46. a train

47. a typist

48. a waitress

49. a watch

50. a window

51. short tall

52. fat thin

53. big little

54. long short

55. thick thin

56. young old

57. old new

58. beautiful ugly

59. dirty clean

60. happy sad

第 二 冊 學 習 內 容 一 覽 表

單元	內　　容	練　　習	活　　動	習　作
複習第一冊	(1)(A)有多少？(B)現在是幾點幾分？ (2)(A)這是什麼？(B)那是什麼？(C)這是我的～ (3)(A)我是／你是～ (B)他是／她是～	Look and say. Look and say. Point and say. Do and say. Look and say.		
1	哈囉，你好嗎？	Look and say：從圖中練習 Hello! How are you？等。	歌曲：Hello, how are you？	本單元注重口說練習
2	現在幾點鐘？(2)	Look and say：從圖中練習 half 和 quarter 的用法	遊戲：What time is it？	Write and draw.
3	你幾歲？你多高？	Questions and answers：練習年齡和身高的問法與答法	歌曲：How old are you？	本單元注重口說練習
4	有一個黑板 有四本書	Point and say：從圖中練習 There is a～. 和 There are～.	遊戲：Say from memory.	Look and write.
5	有一個房子嗎？ 有兩隻狗嗎？	Questions and answers：從圖中練習 Is there a～？的問與答	遊戲：Do and say.	Look, answer and draw.
6	星期與月份	Learn these rhymes：從兩首詩歌中練習星期與月份的說法	歌曲：Days of a week	Fill in the blanks.
7	它是什麼？	Look and say：從猜謎遊戲中熟練 it 的用法	歌曲：Is this a book？	Join, write and say. Draw and write.
8	這些是梨子 那些是梨子	Look and say：從圖中各種遠近不同的事物來練習These are～. 和 Those are～.	遊戲：Hangman	Look at the pictures and make sentences.
9	這些是什麼？ 那些是什麼？	Questions and answers：練習What are these？They are～.	遊戲：Hit the bat.	Write and read.
10	你的爸爸做什麼？	Questions and answers：認識各種職業名稱	遊戲：A crossword puzzle.	Make sentences.
11	顏色(1)： 紅、黃、綠、藍、白、黑、紫	Circle and say：練習 This～(物) is～(顏色). 和 That～(物) is～(顏色).	歌曲：What color is for you？	Color and write.
12	顏色(2)： 棕、粉紅、橘、灰	Look and say：從各物體練習What color is～(物)？	歌曲：Colors	Read and color.
13	尺寸： 大小、長短、高矮、胖瘦、厚薄	Three rhymes：從三首有趣的詩歌中練習 little, long, short 等	歌曲：This little pig went to market.	Circle and read.
14	形容詞：髒的，乾淨的，老的，年輕的，渴的，舊的，新的，…等	Questions and answers：從各種表情中練習 Are you～？(形容詞)及Yes, No 的答法	遊戲：Bring me a new eraser	Look and draw. Make sentences.
複習	看圖練習 看圖練習 看圖練習 生字總複習	Point and say. Look and write. Look, draw and color. Picture dictionary.		